Hurry Up!

by Ann Bryant

Illustrated by Terry Pastor

Crabtree Publishing Company
www.crabtreebooks.com

Crabtree Publishing Company
www.crabtreebooks.com
1-800-387-7650

616 Welland Ave.
St. Catharines, ON
L2M 5V6

PMB 59051, 350 Fifth Ave.
59th Floor,
New York, NY

Published by Crabtree Publishing in 2011

Series Editor: Jackie Hamley
Editors: Melanie Palmer, Reagan Miller
Series Advisor: Catherine Glavina
Series Designer: Peter Scoulding
Project Coordinator: Kathy Middleton

Text © Ann Bryant 2010
Illustration © Terry Pastor 2010

Printed in Hong Kong/042011/BK20110304

First published in 2010
by Franklin Watts
(A division of Hachette
Children's Books)

The rights of the author and the
illustrator of this Work have
been asserted.

Library and Archives Canada
Cataloguing in Publication

Bryant, Ann
　　Hurry up! / by Ann Bryant ; illustrated by Terry
Pastor.

(Tadpoles)
ISBN 978-0-7787-0580-2 (bound).--
ISBN 978-0-7787-0591-8 (pbk.)

　　I. Pastor, Terry II. Title. III. Series: Tadpoles
(St. Catharines, Ont.)

PZ7.B873Hu 2011　　　　j823'.914　　　　C2011-900155-1

Library of Congress
Cataloging-in-Publication Data

Bryant, Ann.
　Hurry up! / by Ann Bryant ; illustrated by Terry
Pastor.
　　　p. cm. -- (Tadpoles)
　Summary: Vehicles of all sorts get angry when they
are stuck behind a slow-moving tractor.
　　ISBN 978-0-7787-0591-8 (pbk. : alk. paper) --
　ISBN 978-0-7787-0580-2 (reinforced library binding :
alk. paper)
　　[1. Tractors--Fiction. 2. Motor vehicles--Fiction.
3. Traffic congestion--Fiction. 4. Patience--Fiction.]
　I. Pastor, Terry, ill. II. Title. III. Series.

PZ7.B8298Hur 2011
[E]--dc22
　　　　　　　　　　2010052366

Here is a list of the words in this story.

Common words:

at	not	up
oh	so	very
no	the	was

Other words:

bus	last	truck
car	slow	turned
corner	taxi	van
hurry	tractor	

The tractor was very slow.

But the car
was in a hurry.

The van was in a hurry.

The taxi was in a hurry.

So was the truck.

The bus was in a very big hurry.

The tractor turned the corner.

At last!

Oh no!

Hurry up tractor!

Puzzle Time

Can you find these pictures in the story?

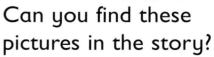

Which pages are
the pictures from?

Turn over for the answers!

Answers

The pictures come from these pages:
a. pages 4 and 5
b. pages 14 and 15
c. pages 8 and 9
d. pages 18 and 19

Notes for adults

Tadpoles are structured to provide support for early readers. The stories may also be used by adults for sharing with young children.

Starting to read alone can be daunting. **Tadpoles** help by listing the words in the book for a preview before reading. **Tadpoles** also provide strong visual support and repeat words and phrases. These books will both develop confidence and encourage reading and rereading for pleasure.

If you are reading this book with a child, here are a few suggestions:

1. Make reading fun! Choose a time to read when you and the child are relaxed and have time to share the story.

2. Look at the picture on the front cover and read the blurb on the back cover. What might the story be about? Why might the child like it?

3. Look at the list of words on page two. Can the child identify most of the words?

4. Encourage the child to retell the story using the jumbled picture puzzle on pages 22-23.

5. Discuss the story and see if the child can relate it to his or her own experiences, or perhaps compare it to another story he or she knows.

6. Give praise! Children learn best in a positive environment.

If you enjoyed this book, why not try another **TADPOLES** story?
Please see the back cover for more **TADPOLES** titles.
Visit **www.crabtreebooks.com** for other **Crabtree** books.